The Fish Bride

The Fish Bride

and Other Gypsy Tales

Retold by Jean Russell Larson

Illustrations by Michael Larson

Linnet Books
North Haven, Connecticut

First published 2000 as a Linnet Book,
an imprint of The Shoe String Press, Inc.
2 Linsley Street, North Haven, Connecticut 06473.

Library of Congress Cataloging-in-Publication Data

Larson, Jean Russell.
  The fish bride and other Gypsy tales / retold by Jean Russell
Larson; illustrations by Michael Larson.
    p. cm.
  Includes bibliographical references.
  Summary: A collection of sixteen Gypsy folktales retold
from the traditions of the Welsh and American Rom. Includes
proverbs and sayings.
  ISBN 0-208-02474-3 (lib. bdg. : alk. paper)
  1. Gypsies--Folklore. 2. Tales--Wales. 3. Tales--United States.
[1. Gypsies--Folklore. 2. Folklore--Wales. 3. Folklore--United
States.] I. Larson, Michael (Michael C.), ill. II. Title.

PZ8.1.L33 Fi 2000
398.2'089'91497--dc21   00-033042

The paper in this publication meets the minimum requirements
of American National Standard for Information Sciences—
Permanence of Paper for Printed Library Materials,
ANSI Z39.48—1984. ∞

Designed by Carol Sawyer of Rose Design

Printed in the United States of America

This book is dedicated to those Gypsy storytellers who brought color and excitement to our small Midwestern community during the bleak years of the Great Depression.

A Gypsy never knows his tomorrow.

Contents

A Gypsy proverb follows each tale.

Introduction

A bean in liberty is better than a cake in prison.
—Gypsy proverb

The beginning of this collection dates from my childhood in the late 1930s. In those days, Gypsies came nearly every summer to my small Iowa hometown and camped near the Iowa River. They went from door to door in the town, selling brightly colored crepe paper flowers. But in those lean years of the Great Depression, sales were few and far between.

On a hot June afternoon, as I sat with neighborhood friends on my front porch, some Gypsy women came down our street, peddling flowers. Two Gypsy girls advanced to my porch. The older of the two carried a basket of flowers which bumped her leg at every step. The younger girl remained behind her, twisting the hem of her faded cotton dress with sweaty fingers.

My mother was not at home, so it fell to me to reject the flowers. But the encounter did not end there. Some of us aimed mean-spirited observations at the two Gypsy girls, echoing old prejudices we had heard from adults.

The two girls did not respond to our taunts, but turned away, leaving us to feel somewhat superior and a little ashamed.

After that the older of the Gypsy girls became a target. Someone heard that her name was Lena, so girls and boys who played in the park adjacent to the Gypsy camp would call Lena's name over and over and even began a game using her name as an object of scorn.

The highlight of the summer was to be the old settlers' picnic, and the families of all the original founders of the community were invited. The picnic would be held in the park on the banks of the river.

After an early morning storm, the sun broke through the clouds, promising a perfect day. A large crowd was in attendance and a basket dinner was planned for noon. As women unpacked chicken pies, bowls of coleslaw, and layer cakes, men played at horseshoes and children hooted up and down the nearby road on foot and on bicycles.

The entertainment that day was presented at the band pavilion in the center of the park. The principal address was given by the pastor of the Methodist chuch, and his remarks about the resolute pioneers of the county fell on appreciative ears.

When the pastor had finished, a local quartet sang a medley of old favorites. Then a sextet, horns at the ready, stepped forward to play. It was at that moment that a remarkable event occurred.

Up over the levee, straight across the green, their aged engines coughing and sputtering, came a parade of battered automobiles. The Gypsies were coming! As the vehicles approached, all the old settlers' celebrants were silent, as though they had been mesmerized.

My friend saw her first.

Introduction

"It's Lena, that Gypsy girl!" she cried, pointing to the back of an ancient touring car.

We all saw her then.

Lena reigned from atop the seat, her delicate chin raised defiantly and her dark eyes fixed on some distant vision of glory we could not hope to share. Her hair spangled in the sunlight.

The dress Lena wore was of plum-colored silk. A jeweled girdle circled her waist. The bracelets on her slender wrists were gold.

I stood with my friends, stunned by Lena's transformation. Which of us would not exchange places with her? Which of us was not bewitched?

For an instant, as her chariot passed, Lena's gaze rested on me and my companions and her eyes glittered dangerously. Then she was gone. The Gypsies had shown us how much they prized her and we were deservedly chastened.

A few of us now ventured to the Gypsy camp and we were not turned away. Why they allowed us there after our disgraceful behavior, I do not know.

When I learned there was storytelling in that camp, nothing could have prevented me from returning. Wherever stories were told, there was I. I came of a long line of storytellers, and for years I kept a handmade notebook containing tales told by my Irish grandfather, my Norwegian grandmother, as well as random stories which reached my ears. The Gypsy tales filled pages, but that childhood notebook is long gone.

Gypsy storytellers depend on an oral tradition instead of the written word. Such a tradition trains both teller and hearer to listen more acutely and to sharpen the memory. Although not schooled in those techniques, I have tried here, without benefit of my childhood book, to recreate those Gypsy tales of long ago.

As I grew older, making myths and folklore a major part of my coursework on both the undergraduate and graduate levels, I recalled those tales told years before by Gypsy storytellers. They were unlike any stories I had studied, for they reflected a deep desire for freedom, a joyful acceptance of the Gypsies' place in the world, and cleverly honed instincts for survival. Yet I was able to identify many motifs in the Gypsy tales and connect them with stories from diverse cultures. Gypsy storytellers are skillful in adapting regional material, already familiar to the listener. Their stories also reflect a desire to delight hearers and they touch with precision the sensitivities of their audience. They give the listener what she wants.

At nearly the same time I was listening, enthralled, to Gypsy stories near the bank of the Iowa River, young Jack Richards was working on a farm above Strata Florida Abbey, near the village of Pontrhydfendigaid in Wales. Jack had known Gypsies all his life. He had listened to tales told by old Jack E., often called the finest Romany gentleman in Wales, and Ben, who came around twice each year with boxes of brooches, necklaces, and needles to sell.

In later years, in a letter, Jack recalled the Gypsies fondly:

> They were honest and trusted. Some of them told
> fortunes and were very accurate and all they asked

was a silver coin. Old Ben was a brilliant scholar and fluent in Welsh. We always welcomed him with a cup of tea.

Over the years, Jack collected those Gypsy tales he heard in his youth, as well as stories in Wales. He was acknowledged by local residents and amateur historians as an authority on folklore. Upon his retirement from the forestry commission, he devoted his time to recalling the old, nearly forgotten stories, as well as to teaching the Welsh language to English speakers.

My daughter, Kathleen, an avid gardener, became acquainted with Jack Richards and his wife Bet in 1981. Jack was also a devoted gardener and a firm friendship developed. The stories Jack delighted in passed to Kathy through letters and in a visit to the Richards' home in Wales. When I heard those stories, the thought began to occur to me that a book might be made, combining Gypsy tales from Wales heard first-hand with the tales told long ago by Gypsies camping in my Iowa hometown. Jack Richards died in 1992, but Bet Richards has generously given permission to include his stories in this collection. They include "The Gypsy Harper," "Jack and the Green Man," "Biddy Oak," "The Haunted Inn," and "The Black Dog."

In due course, I learned something about the Gypsies or, as they call themselves, Rom, meaning "the People." Coming originally from the Indian subcontinent they began spreading over the Near East and arriving in Europe in the 1400s. They earned a living by horse-dealing, fortunetelling, craft work, and entertaining. Their beautiful music and dance are legendary. But nearly everywhere they went, the Rom were feared and hated as different from settled people, and were driven on. They have been described as being in the world but not of the world, since they are fiercely loyal to their own traditions and codes of conduct. Theirs is a male-ordered society, centered on the family, tribe, and clan.

For centuries Gypsies have suffered persecution, expulsion from various lands, and death. Thousands died as victims of the Nazis in World War II. Today, the Rom can be found in almost every part of the world. Up to an estimated twelve million are living outside India, about one million of these in the United States. Many of these people are settled, following professions, trades, and various occupations. Many more, especially those in Europe, continue the wandering lifestyle of their ancestors.

Gypsy stories, similar to fairy tales in other cultures, are told for entertainment and amusement. These tales are set in the long-ago and far-away and often contain magical objects, supernatural adversaries, and mysterious transformations.

Examples here of such stories are "The Starry Loom," which is set in a time when anything could happen and usually did, and carries a luckless heroine up among the stars to the gates of time. Another of these is "Lallah Pombo," in which a simple Gypsy girl sets out to overcome an evil magician's curse. This story takes place in the first days following the long darkness.

"Jack and the Green Man," a story from Wales, is an example of a "foolish Jack" tale, and contains elements of a fairy tale. "Noodle" and "Clever Marco" also feature foolish young men, but fall into a second category of Gypsy stories, those of cautionary tales told to instruct and to serve as warnings in an often hostile world. "King of the Moon," in which we again meet Marco, falls into this category, pitting the young Gypsy against a wily czar.

Storytelling continues today among the Gypsies. Traditional themes and motifs are still employed, while variants and new stories are created. The telling of tales is, for Gypsy people, a lively art. The importance of preserving folktales and folk wisdom cannot be overstated, for such lore is both culture-bearing and values-laden and deserves to be cherished. As the Gypsies say, "The best is soonest gone."

Gypsies have traditionally scorned the values of settled *gadje* (non-Gypsies), preferring the freedom of the open road. In this tale, Piccolo finds true joy in the life of a wanderer, singing and dancing. Gypsy melodies are among the world's most beautiful. According to an old saying, "A Gypsy's heart is made of music."

Piccolo

Long ago, far over the water, the people of a certain town were sober and industrious. They busied themselves every day, baking serious bread, making proper cheese, and raising well-behaved onions and peppers. These people were very proud of themselves.

But the citizens of that town never sang or danced and they had forgotten how to laugh. God was displeased with them because they were vain and as sour as vinegar.

One night, as he slept, God had a dream. In that dream, he saw a Gypsy boy capering and dancing in fast shoes, bringing laughter to all who saw him.

At dawn, when dreams turn into reality, God brought that Gypsy boy to life. He dressed him in a coat with bright patches, a soft hat, and fast shoes.

1

"Go and dance, because that is what I made you for," God said, setting the boy on the road to the town.

The Gypsy boy started down the road, then turned and called to God.

"What is my name?" he asked.

"You are Piccolo, because you are a little bit of nothing," God chuckled.

Piccolo arrived in the town and went straightaway to the market square. The sun shone brightly and the square was crowded with shoppers.

Piccolo chose a spot before a fruit vendor's stall and began to dance, singing a merry tune and clapping his hands.

Passers-by stared at him in horror.

"Stop at once!" the fruit vendor cried.

Piccolo stopped.

"I can see you are a stranger here, so I will give you good advice," the fruit vendor said. "You must not dance like a fool, but behave as others do. If you do not, you will have no friends. It is clear you do not understand how things work in this world."

Piccolo excused himself and hurried from the town and down the road to the place he had left God.

There was God.

Piccolo addressed him politely. "You do not understand how things work in this world," he said. "I cannot dance and caper about. If I am not like everyone else, I will have no friends."

God said gently, "I am your friend. Go and dance."

Piccolo

Piccolo returned to the town square, selected a spot before the stall of a baker who was selling very serious bread, and began to dance.

"Stop at once!" the baker cried. "Because you are new here, I will give you good advice. If you hold your head high and smile at no one, you will be considered a fine fellow. You will gain respect. By dancing like a fool, you are making a mistake."

Piccolo listened carefully, then excused himself and hastened from the town to the place where he had left God.

There was God.

"See here," Piccolo called as he approached, "you have made a mistake. If I dance and act the fool, I will get no respect."

God sighed, then said patiently, "I made you to dance. If you do not do as I say, you will not respect yourself."

Piccolo scowled. It was clear to him that God did not know what he was talking about.

Again Piccolo entered the town. This time, he stopped before the stall of an onion vendor and began to dance half-heartedly, seeing frowns on the faces of all the passers-by.

"Stop that foolish dancing, you good-for-nothing boy," the onion vendor ordered. "Go and earn an honest living or you will starve. You don't know anything!"

The crowd that had gathered hooted and jeered at Piccolo.

Piccolo hid his face in shame and sped from the town to confront God.

God was there.

"You don't know anything!" Piccolo shouted. "If I dance, I will starve!"

"Then starve!" roared God, for he was out of patience.

Piccolo was bewildered.

God would say no more, so Piccolo turned and walked slowly toward the town, trying hard to understand all that had happened.

But as he went, it seemed to Piccolo that he heard music, as if from some far-off place, beyond the horizon. Though he tried to step along in a dignified manner, he could not keep his fast shoes from dancing, so that by the time he reached the town he was dancing and singing and snapping his fingers like castanets.

Even before Piccolo reached the market square, a line of children had formed behind him, and all of them danced as if they heard the music, too.

It would be pleasant to report that all the townspeople changed their sour ways for songs and laughter. That was not the case. Many years passed before music was once again heard in that town.

But Piccolo went from place to place, capering and dancing, and God smiled on him.

God knows what tomorrow will bring.

In traditional Gypsy culture, young girls are expected to stay at home. In this cautionary tale, a willful Gypsy girl encounters a wise old woman and her magic loom, motifs found in the folklore of many lands.

The Starry Loom

There was once a time when anything could happen, and usually did. At that time, a Gypsy girl called Sikri, who was willful and vain, was returning to her caravan at midnight when she fell through a crack in time.

Sikri tumbled upward, around and around, landing at last at the feet of an old woman who sat weaving. The loom upon which she wove was set with stars; the spindle and shuttle were silver.

"What place is this and who are you?" Sikri demanded.

The old woman spoke without taking her eyes from her work.

"I am the spinster who sits at the gates of time. I am as old as the world. I weave a pattern each day upon this loom, then that pattern takes shape upon the earth. I weave each night in the same way."

"I am no fool," Sikri snapped. "If you weave patterns for days and nights, then you must know the future before it happens."

"That is so," the old woman agreed.

Sikri peered closely at the pattern on the loom.

"You are weaving a picture of this night, and I am in it, rising into the heavens," Sikri cried.

"When you should have been at home in bed," the old woman said. "But you were abroad at the midnight hour because you are willful and obey no one."

Sikri sat down to think about the great mystery she had stumbled upon.

The old woman continued to weave, her fingers darting like spiders over the loom. All about her, a wild wind blew and darkness covered the earth below.

Sikri looked at the old woman and determined to get the best of her.

"See here, I want the power to weave the future and I want it now!" Sikri said.

"You do not realize what you are saying," the old woman replied.

For three days and three nights Sikri disputed with the old woman. She tried every trick she knew: tricks that had never failed her before. She pleaded, she wept, and she threatened. But the old woman reamined firm, continuing to weave.

7

The Fish Bride

At last, losing all patience, Sikri pushed the old woman aside and sat down at the loom, grasping the shuttle.

"I always get what I want!" Sikri announced.

"And so you shall, now," the old woman said, smiling slyly.

But when Sikri tried to loosen her hold on the shuttle, her hand clung fast. And struggle as she would, she could not rise from the loom.

The old woman wrapped her cloak close about her and started down the sky.

"Where are you going?" Sikri screamed.

"Wherever the wind blows me. The world is always in need of a wise woman," the old woman called over her shoulder.

That is how it came about that a Gypsy girl sits at the gates of time, weaving upon the starry loom.

The buyer needs a hundred eyes,
the seller but one.

Fables, animal tales told with an acknowledged moral purpose, are not common in Gypsy literature. This fable features a lion, symbol of strength, and a fox, that universal trickster who has found his way into the stories of many lands. But the victor here is a clever bird, whose efforts to outwit the powerful reflect the Gypsies' own struggles in a hostile world.

The Lion, the Fox, and the Bird

Once a lion and a fox went to live in a certain forest. There dwelled in that forest a bird which was plump and slow of wing.

"You should leave this place at once," the bird was advised by his friends. "Go and seek shelter far from here, for the lion with his strength will overcome you and devour you; and if he does not, the cunning fox will make a meal of you."

But the bird was not afraid. He said to his friends, "Where would I find another home so fine? I shall not leave. Instead I shall force the lion and the fox to go."

At this the bird's friends laughed and called him a fool.

Now the lion had seen the plump bird, and he said to the fox, "That bird will be a good mouthful."

"You will never taste it," the fox replied, "for I mean to eat it myself."

Whereupon the lion roared with anger and said, "You cannot match my strength. The bird will be mine!"

"You cannot match my wits," the fox replied. "The bird will be mine!"

And it happened, as the lion and the fox disputed between themselves, that the bird flew down from a tall tree and addressed them.

"Oh sirs," he said, "how happy I am that you have come here, for I am in need of food and can find none."

Now the lion and the fox were surprised to see the bird standing before them in this manner. The lion thought to pounce upon the bird, but it would have been shameful to kill a creature who had come to ask for help.

"What can we do for you?" the fox asked.

The bird looked to the left.

"There are berries there, in the thicket," he said, "and my mouth waters for the taste of them, but I cannot reach the bushes."

"Why is that?" the lion asked.

"The bushes are caught beneath some fallen trees," the bird answered, "and I have not strength enough to free them."

"That is no problem," the lion said and straightaway he went among the trees, pushing them aside with his mighty paws until the berry bushes were uncovered.

The bird then feasted upon the berries until he had his fill, thanked the lion politely, and went on his way.

"Why did you help him?" the fox asked.

"What else could I do," the lion pleaded, "when he laid his problem at my very feet? He needed me."

On the following day, as the lion and the fox walked among the trees, the bird came again to them.

"How happy I am to see you!" he said. "I need your help once again."

"What is it this time?" the lion asked.

The bird looked to the right, where the wide river flowed.

"There, in the river," he said, "are some tall reeds that would make a fine nest. But I am not suited by nature to enter the water and so I cannot gather the reeds."

"That is no problem," said the cunning fox. Whereupon he went forward to the river and addressed himself to a group of herons standing on the bank.

"Look how those reeds cloud the water," he pointed out. "If the reeds were gone, you would spot juicy fish more clearly."

Seeing the wisdom of the fox's words, the herons made haste to pull up the reeds with their beaks and place them on the riverbank.

"There are your reeds," said the fox to the bird. "Now you may build your nest."

"Why did you help him?" the lion asked, when the bird had gone.

"I could do nothing else when he laid his problem at my very feet," the fox answered. "He needed me."

It was but a day later when the bird came again to the lion and the fox. "How happy I am to see you, sirs," he said, "for I must ask your help once again."

"What is it now?" growled the fox. How he longed to spring upon the bird and make a meal of him! But it would have been shameful to kill a creature who had come looking for help.

"There are those in this forest who would kill me and eat me," the bird said, making a sad face. "As you are my friends, I ask your protection."

"This is too much!" the fox cried. "You come to us for food and for shelter. Now you ask for our protection. You know well who it is who wants to eat you, and you have made us powerless by trusting us."

Then the lion and the fox left the forest and went where they might hunt food more fairly.

"How did you force them to go?" the bird was asked by his friends.

"Remember, there is great strength in weakness," the bird replied.

Call the bear "uncle" until you are safe across the bridge.

A common folk theme is one in which a simple, kind-hearted young man meets a trickster. In many cases, goodness triumphs. But sometimes the foolish lad gains only experience.

Noodle

There once lived a Gypsy boy who was called Noodle because he was very fool-ish. Noodle's mother dressed him in a fine coat and shiny boots and sent him to town to sell honey cakes. She believed he would succeed, since he was the apple of her eye.

But Noodle was not a good salesman and he left the town with his bag of honey cakes and a heavy heart.

Noodle's way home took him through a dark forest and as he walked, he heard the sound of someone moaning. Within a few steps, he came across an old man, sitting on a tree stump and sobbing bitterly by the light of the moon.

"I wonder if you would tell me what the trouble is," Noodle said.

"I have lost a purse filled with rubles and cannot go home until I find it," the old man wailed. He clutched the sleeve of Noodle's coat. "Heaven must have sent you to help me."

Now Noodle was foolish, but he knew one or two things and he became suspicious.

"I will need proof of what you tell me before I agree to help you," he said cautiously.

"That is the easiest thing in the world," the old man replied. "I can tell you exactly how many rubles were in that purse. There were twenty-seven."

Noodle thought hard about that, and decided he could trust such an intelligent fellow. Poor Noodle did not know there are tricksters in this world who outwit foolish boys.

Noodle and the old man began to search the ground, but they had not gone far when the old man advised, "Set down your bag, young Gypsy, so you may use both hands to look among the fallen leaves."

Noodle placed his bag of honey cakes on the ground beside a tree. The two began to search.

They had not gone far when the old man said, "Let us remove our shoes so we do not tread upon the purse."

The old man removed his broken shoes and Noodle removed his shiny boots. They began again to look for the purse.

They had not gone many steps when the old man suggested, "Let us remove our coats so we may move more freely." Then he took off his tattered coat and placed it on the ground.

Noodle removed his fine coat and placed it beside the raggedy one.

They walked a little farther, and then the old man paused and seemed to consider. "Continue on," he urged, "and I will retrace our steps in case we have overlooked the purse."

Noodle thought that very wise, so he continued on.

The old man retraced their steps, putting on Noodle's fine coat, his shiny boots, and picking up his bag of honey cakes as he went.

Then he was on his way, smiling.

Noodle returned to his home, poorer but a little wiser.

If a donkey goes traveling, he'll not come home a horse.

The "evil eye" was greatly feared by the Gypsies who used the superstition to account for illnesses, the sudden disappearance of people, or the inexplicable accidents that happened to them. This came about as a glance from the person—in this case, Magda, a sort of living dead figure—who was associated with the underworld. Victims of the evil eye were said to be "overlooked" or "evil-seen" and the effects were countered with garlic, mixtures such as coals, meal, and garlic boiled in spring water, as well as rhymes and incantations.

The Evil Eye

Magda had the evil eye. Everyone in the town and around said so. She did not belong in this world, but in the nether world. The people of the town turned her out and she vowed to get even with them.

One summer night, Magda was struck by a bolt of lightning and appeared to die. Everyone rejoiced, but they did not rejoice long, for Magda had only slipped into the nether world and she returned in just a few days.

From time to time thereafter, Magda was seen along roadsides and at crossroads. Using her evil eye, she lured unwary travelers into deep bogs and poisonous lakes.

A cry went up from the people that the roads must be made safe, but each time someone attempted to catch Magda, she slipped into the nether world.

One day, a farm girl strolled into a meadow, leaving her work undone. The thought came into her silly head to weave a ring of flowers.

Magda appeared on the scene. She said never a word, but lured the girl, by means of her evil eye, to a well near at hand and pushed her in.

A cow doctor, riding home in the twilight, encountered Magda at the top of a very high hill and was sent heels over head, tumbling down.

A girl selling young nettles in the market was led into a very disagreeable tar pit.

Magda went one day to a coffeehouse and there spied some gentlemen playing cards. She took notice of a boastful fellow who wore a checkered coat and a feather in his hat. Magda knew at once that she did not like him.

Lifting the hood of her cloak just enough to reveal her evil eye, Magda lured the boastful card player out of the coffeehouse to a trackless marsh.

Time passed and after a while people began to notice that many from the town and around had disappeared.

"It is the work of Magda," they all agreed. But every attempt to catch her failed.

Magda grew bolder. She began to seek out victims in their own homes, despite locks on the doors. She went in at the windows and down through the chimneys. She lured women away as they peeled onions for goulash or men as they mended harness for their horses. No one was safe.

Believing kindness might provide a solution to the problem, townspeople began to leave baskets of food at the crossroads for Magda, but cheese and pastry did not content her. Once, when she came at sunset to drink from a cream bowl, a young man crept from the trees and tried to capture her, but after a fierce struggle, Magda vanished.

Now, Fate had been watching all of this. One morning, as Magda was on her way to gather children and lose them in the forest, she came to a bridge to admire her reflection in the water. There was her evil eye, looking up at her, beckoning her into the river.

For a very long time, people feared Magda would return, and they were careful not to disturb the water, because you never can tell.

Nice reeds make nice baskets.

In this tale, a young girl's generosity is a reflection of her compassion. Her kindness is observed and rewarded, illustrating the Gypsy saying, "God is to be found in the forest, not in the church."

Lichka

A young girl called Lichka was left alone in her lonely cottage when her brother went to his army service. Winter came on and a great storm arose, driving snow round and round outside the cottage.

Lichka could not go to town for food, for she had no way of traveling and no money, in any case. Soon there would be only a cabbage, two onions, and three potatoes in the bin.

Each day Lichka worked at making a new cloak for herself. Her old one was full of holes.

On the night Lichka cooked the cabbage over her peat fire, came three knocks on her door. An old Gypsy woman, drenched and dripping, blew in, leaning on a stout walking stick.

"What comfort will you offer an old woman on this blustery night?" the Gypsy asked.

20

Lichka

"The welcome of a peat fire and a bowl of cabbage soup are yours, old mother," Lichka replied kindly.

The old woman warmed herself by the fire, and then ate all of the cabbage, leaving none for Lichka.

"You will find a reward for your kindness," the Gypsy said, and left.

The storm raged on and a fierce wind sought out chinks in the cottage walls.

The next night, as Lichka cooked the two onions over a peat fire, came three knocks on the cottage door. Once again the old Gypsy woman blew in, drenched and dripping, leaning on her stick.

"What comfort for an old woman this night?" she asked.

"The welcome of a peat fire and a bowl of onion soup, old mother," Lichka offered.

The old Gypsy warmed herself before the fire and ate all of the onion soup, leaving none for Lichka.

"You will find a reward for your kindness," said the Gypsy, and left.

Next day, at twilight, Lichka finished sewing her warm cloak. She put it aside and cooked the three potatoes over a peat fire.

Just as before, three knocks came on the door and in blew the old Gypsy, leaning on her stick.

"What welcome this night?" she asked.

"The warmth of a fire and a soup of potatoes, old mother," Lichka answered kindly, though now she was near starvation herself.

The Gypsy sat before the fire, eating the soup. She ate it

all and left none for Lichka.

Then she spied Lichka's new cloak and tried it around her own shoulders. "This cloak would warm me on the road," she observed.

"Take it and welcome, old mother," Lichka offered. But before the words were out of her mouth, the Gypsy had gone out into the night leaving her walking stick behind.

Now there was no food in the bin and Lichka's new cloak was gone.

The next night, just as before, three knocks came on the door. Thinking the Gypsy must be there, Lichka opened the door.

Outside was a three-headed monster with gaping jaws and six eyes, burning like coals. Terrified, Lichka tried to close her door, but the monster pushed it open.

Seeing the Gypsy's stout stick beside the door, Lichka seized it and brought it down hard upon the largest of the monster's heads.

In a flash the monster vanished and in its place stood a sturdy horse, hitched to a shiny cart. At that moment, a shower of gold coins rained down on Lichka.

As the Gypsy foretold, Lichka's kindness was rewarded. From that day on, she lived in wealth and cheer.

Behind bad luck comes good luck.

Here is Marco, the young Gypsy who believes himself smarter than everyone else in the world. Marco represents a stock figure in Gypsy literature. Unlike the character Jack, who is plucky, or foolish Noodle, Marco is a lad with an eye to the main chance. He appears again in the story "King of the Moon."

Clever Marco

Once an old Gypsy widow had a foolish son called Marco. This Marco believed himself to be very clever. One day, he said to his mother, "I have decided that I am smarter than everyone else in the world."

"Take care," his mother warned. "One of these days someone will outwit you."

"That day will never come," Marco scoffed. Then he set out alone to find good luck.

Two sisters, Hannah and Minnie Gluck, lived in a small cottage on an acre of ground near the River Tisza. The sisters took produce from their large garden and eggs from their poultry to market, and they prospered. But the Gluck sisters were not satisfied. They were a greedy pair whose aim in life was to become rich.

Winter came early that year. Frost covered the ground and birds huddled near cottage chimneys to keep warm.

On a blustery day, Marco hurried down a country road. He wore flimsy clothes, a broken hat, and carried a traveling bag over his shoulder. Marco's one aim in life on that cold, cold day was to eat without working for the meal.

Marco surveyed the Gluck sisters' home, from the thatched roof to the whitewashed walls and the pen of fat honking geese nearby, and smiled.

"I'm sure to find a good meal here," he thought. Then he began to calculate how he could while away a few pleasant days there.

Marco rapped at the cottage door.

Now the Gluck sisters had not prospered by being fools. They were sharp as needles. The sisters took one look at Marco with his kerchief around his neck and his bag slung over his shoulder and made up their minds he was a rich Gypsy. They then began to figure how they could separate Marco from his money.

"I will be grateful if you will lend me a drink of water," Marco said, tipping his hat.

"We will be proud to lend you a drink," Hannah replied, pumping Marco's hand heartily.

"Come in and warm your shins by the fire," Minnie urged.

Marco saw Hannah and Minnie eyeing his traveling bag and guessed they thought money was in it. So he made up his mind to outsmart them. He took off his hat, but he did not remove the bag from his shoulder.

"We are about to sit down to the evening meal and will be pleased to have you join us," Hannah said.

Marco craned his neck to see what was cooking. Cabbage. "I'm not fond of cabbage," he said. "I favor goulash."

So Hannah and Minnie set to work at once, browning meat and slicing onions for goulash.

Marco took a seat at the table and set himself up for business. As the goulash was handed around, Marco and the Gluck sisters began to get acquainted.

"Are you a fiddler or a horse trader, neighbor Marco?" Minnie asked.

"I don't favor horse-trading, and fiddlers are a pitiful lot," Marco said, helping himself to the goulash. "I am what is known as a thinker."

"A thinker!" Hannah cried. "That's wonderful!"

"Is there any money in thinking, neighbor Marco?" Minnie asked slyly.

"Is there any money in thinking?" Marco echoed in an astonished voice. "Why, I've been thinking since I was no taller than a goose's knee and I can truthfully say I have never missed a meal." He spread cheese on a thick slice of dark bread and took an enormous bite.

When the meal was finished, Hannah and Minnie washed the pots and pans, while Marco entertained them by singing Gypsy songs and playing with their old dog Fritz.

"You must be worn down from traveling, neighbor Marco," Minnie observed. "You are welcome to spend the night in the shed behind our cottage, where there is a straw mattress."

"Oh, I can't sleep in a shed, where I would surely catch cold," Marco said. "That would hinder my thinking."

Matters were soon settled and Marco nestled down with two feather ticks before the cottage fireplace. The fire had been banked for the night. Marco pillowed his head on his traveling bag and went to sleep with a satisfied mind, because he was out-smarting the Gluck sisters.

Now Minnie Gluck had an eye for snooping. At midnight, while Hannah dreamed dreams of getting rich, Minnie crept from her bed. She planned to see what was in Marco's traveling bag. But Marco expected company and he slept with one eye open.

Minnie came creeping.

Marco heard her approach and when she was beside his bed, he called out in a sudden voice, "Who's there?"

Minnie stepped backward in surprise and stepped on the tail of old Fritz, who lay by the embers.

Fritz howled and struggled to get up, bumping into a large clock and knocking it over.

The clock fell on Minnie's foot and she began to yell.

Hannah awoke with a start. Thinking robbers had entered the cottage, she stumbled out of bed shouting for help.

Minnie clutched her foot and danced in a circle, colliding with Hannah. The two fell on Fritz and he joined in the uproar.

Marco chuckled softly to himself and slept.

"What was all the commotion last night?" Marco asked the next morning.

"Never mind!" Minnie snapped.

Clever Marco

The Gluck sisters spared no effort in cooking and baking that day. They were determined to make Marco comfortable until they could sneak that travel bag away from him.

"If you will bring in a little firewood, neighbor Marco, I'll set a pot of sausage and sauerkraut on for dinner," Hannah said.

Marco carried load after load of firewood into the cottage and kept the fire blazing.

Minnie cleaned the cottage, wielding a feather duster with a flourish. "If you will just move the table and chairs, neighbor Marco, I'll sweep behind them," she said.

Marco was so proud to be outsmarting the Gluck sisters that he hardly noticed how heavy the furniture was.

At dinner, Hannah said, "I guess this food doesn't measure up to the meals you are accustomed to, neighbor Marco."

Marco helped himself to a sausage. "This is pleasant enough," he said, with a smile of sweet charity.

Hannah and Minnie stole sidelong glances at Marco's traveling bag and speculated on what was in it.

"There might be gold in that old bag," Minnie whispered.

"I heard about a Gypsy who carried around a sackful of jewels," Hannah hissed.

Marco basked in the glow of the Gluck sisters' hospitality.

"Since you are a thinker, will you favor us with a little thinking, neighbor Marco?" Hannah asked.

Marco ate a bite of sauerkraut, then smiled. "I've been thinking that a cottage is warmer than an open road."

"Speaking of bags...that's a handsome bag you carry," Minnie said. "I wonder what might be inside it."

"Why, a fortune in gold might fit inside it," Hannah suggested.

"Maybe it would and maybe it wouldn't," replied Marco.

Later, the Gluck sisters took Marco for a stroll around their acre. A cold wind blew.

"This place is nothing but trouble," Minnie grumbled. "Only this morning the old wooden well-bucket fell to pieces. Somebody will have to tie the new bucket onto the rope."

Marco was full of good will. "Just lead me to that well. I'll tie on that bucket," he promised.

They went at once to the well, where the new bucket sat. Marco sized up the situation. When Hannah and Minnie returned to the cottage, he hauled up the well-rope and found the remains of the old bucket. Then he set the new bucket beside him while he undid the old one.

But Marco was not handy at a job of work because he was out of practice. His fingers were cold and stiff. When he tried to untie the knot in the rope, his elbows sawed the air and one of them collided with the new bucket, pushing it into the well. Marco made a grab for it, but he was too late. He lost his balance and fell into the well.

Marco began to yell.

Minnie and Hannah laid down their mending and hurried from the cottage. They peered into the well.

"Why do you suppose he went down in the well?" Minnie asked.

Hannah shrugged.

"Are you thinking down there, neighbor Marco?" she asked.

"Get me out of here!" Marco howled.

"Hand up your traveling bag to us so it won't get soaked," Minnie suggested. But Marco held fast to his bag and was hauled, dripping wet, from the well.

Marco was exhausted from carrying firewood, moving furniture, and falling into the well. But he wasn't too tired to fold his traveling bag under his head when he settled down to sleep that night. He knew that bag was the reason he was inside a warm cottage, eating like a king.

Day came again. The sight of breakfast on the table was as pleasant as flowers to Marco.

"Cooking as good as this ought to be against the law," Marco cried jovially. "I'll never be satisfied with plain food again."

"We are proud to have you visiting us," Minnie purred. "It isn't every day a thinker comes down the road."

"Speaking of bags," Hannah said, "I wonder if that bag of yours would hold a pound of gold?"

"Maybe it would and maybe it wouldn't," said Marco. He chuckled to himself. "They'll need to get up before daylight to put one over on me," he thought smugly.

Marco was tired from eating his breakfast, so he settled down for a nap. When next he opened his eyes, he found the fire out and the cottage cold.

Hannah and Minnie stood glum-faced.

"The chimney won't draw," Minnie explained.

"It wants cleaning," Hannah added.

Now Marco was not fond of work, but he was hungry for a hot dinner.

"I'm not afraid to go down that chimney," he declared. "Lead me to it."

Armed with a straw broom for cleaning, Marco clambered up the side of the cottage and onto the roof.

"You must be proud of this fine chimney," he called down to Hannah and Minnie.

"It's handsome, but it's troublesome," Minnie replied. "This is the third time this year it has been stopped up. We are grateful for your help, neighbor Marco."

"I'll need a mouthful of teeth for this job," Marco thought, taking the broom in his mouth and scaling the chimney.

At first, all went well. Marco swept the sides of the enormous chimney, sending out a cloud of soot. But halfway down, he became wedged sideways and couldn't wiggle loose. "I'm stuck!" he howled.

"Try thinking," Minnie suggested. "Why, I'll bet you have never done any thinking in a chimney."

"No good ever came of working," Marco snarled. He let go of the broom and it clattered to the hearth below. Then, as he wriggled and squirmed to free himself, the traveling bag fell from his shoulder.

The bag landed on the hearth with a *plop*.

That was the moment the Gluck sisters had waited for. They pounced on the bag together and Minnie snatched it from Hannah.

"Nothing!" Minnie screeched. "This bag is full of nothing!"

Hannah snatched the bag, turned it upside down, and shook it.

Marco worked himself loose and slid down the chimney. He was covered with soot and doubled over with laughter.

"That's right!" he brayed. "You have been cooking and baking and being polite to me all for a bagful of nothing. I outsmarted you!"

Hannah threw the bag on the floor and stomped up and down on it. But Minnie just stood there squinching up her face and staring hard at Marco.

"Neighbor Marco, you are not the only thinker here," she said. "I'm doing some thinking now and it appears to me that we have outsmarted you. You have slept in a warm cottage and have eaten good meals, but we have had our chimney cleaned, firewood gathered, well-bucket fixed, and furniture moved. Looks to me like *we* got the best of *you*."

Marco studied hard on that for a long moment. Then he slung his bag over his shoulder, brushed the soot from his clothes, and started down the road. As he hurried along, considering all that had happened to him, he decided he was not smarter than everyone else in the world.

Anywhere I fall is where I make my bed.

This story is an example of a motif very common in folktales, that of an innocent young girl overpowered by a vain, jealous queen. Here is a blurring of human and supernatural worlds. The transformation of Sita into a small golden fish is reminiscent of the enchantment and burial of the girl Bidasari's soul in the ancient Malaysian epic of that name. While the story may have been Indian in origin, there is in it a strong suggestion of Malaysian influence.

The Fish Bride

In a far corner of the world, long ago, a mysterious shadowy realm was ruled by an evil queen. Some Gypsies, who had left their homeland and journeyed south, lingered there and from time to time one of their number returned up the long and winding road to tell tales of strange occurrences. What follows is one of those tales as it was told by a Gypsy who was there and saw it all. Jungle now obscures the road to that realm and travelers no longer pass that way.

The Fish Bride

The wicked queen, whose name was Rangda, persecuted the Gypsies, causing them great suffering. One of the Gypsies, an old woman famed as a seer, counseled the others to bear the wrongs patiently and wait for a change of fortune, which she assured them would come.

One night, Queen Rangda dreamed a strange dream. In it, she saw a full moon fall to Earth. When no one at the royal court could explain the meaning of the dream, the queen summoned the old Gypsy seer to say what the dream meant.

"Your dream signifies that a beautiful girl child has been born in this realm," the Gypsy said. "She is fair as a flower and will someday sit on your throne."

The queen, who was as vain and jealous as she was wicked, flew into a rage.

"I'm a beauty and a queen. I have no equal in this world!" she cried.

Then Queen Rangda dispatched messengers to all parts of the realm to search for the newborn baby and bring her to the palace.

"I don't like where this is leading," the old Gypsy mused. "I will stay close and see what I can see."

Three years passed before the messengers located the child, a small Gypsy girl named Sita, and returned to the palace with her.

When she saw how beautiful the child was and how like a gracious princess she behaved, the queen became a madwoman, roaring like thunder.

Now the queen knew a spell or two. In a flash, she transformed the innocent child into a small golden fish. In those days, such things did not take much effort. The queen placed the fish in a little teakwood chest and commanded her servants to bury it in the palace garden.

"Ah ha! Here is my chance," the old Gypsy said to herself.

As soon as the earth closed over the teakwood chest, and the servants went away, the Gypsy dug up the chest and slipped the little golden fish into a nearby pool.

Things went on as usual. Sixteen times the orchards flowered, then leaves fluttered and fell. Sixteen times, the wind brought the rain. The Gypsy family grieved for their lost daughter and Queen Rangda continued her wicked ways. The old Gypsy watched over the little golden fish in the pool.

After a while, the spell Queen Rangda had cast over Sita began to fade, and it weakened first at the midnight hour. That is the hour which, itself, possessed powerful magic. And so, at each midnight, Sita was able to rise from the pool and walk in the garden as her true self. The old Gypsy knew this and began to make plans.

Now Queen Rangda had one child, a son who was as good as his mother was evil. Each morning, he studied with a learned scholar, and then spent hours doing kind deeds.

As the time approached when the prince should marry, the queen summoned prospective brides to the palace. From far and wide they came, dressed in finery and fluttering jeweled fans. Families had spared no expense in outfitting their daughters.

When the queen and the prince stepped out to greet the prospective brides, the young women were all wild with excitement and flew about like birds, bumping into one another.

Some of them wiggled their ears and others twitched their noses, hoping to be noticed.

None of them pleased the prince.

One night, the prince dreamed that the full moon fell to Earth, as the old Gypsy knew he would. She hastened to speak to him.

"If you walk in the palace garden at midnight, the meaning of your strange dream will soon be revealed," she promised.

The prince did as the Gypsy said. He walked in the palace garden that very night. At the stroke of midnight, Sita slipped from the pool and revealed her true identity.

As soon as he saw Sita, the prince fell in love with her, because that was the way things happened in that place.

Each night after that, Sita and the prince walked together in the garden, but Sita always sent the prince away before the spell overcame her and she became a fish once more.

Then came the moment for which the old Gypsy had waited. She sent to the queen and demanded that the bride-price be paid to the parents of the young woman the prince had decided to marry.

"Who is the prince's choice and why do you speak for the parents?" the queen demanded.

The Gypsy beckoned the queen and all the courtiers to follow her to the garden pool.

"There is the prince's bride," the Gypsy announced, pointing to the little fish.

The prince was astonished. The courtiers rocked with laughter. But the queen flew into a rage. She ordered the Gypsy to be banished, but the prince, who trusted the Gypsy for her

36

wise counsel, ordered the marriage ceremony to be conducted at once.

The very instant Sita's destiny was fulfilled, she stood revealed as her true self.

Then the queen, who saw she had been defeated by Fate, gave up her throne to the prince and his bride and took up residence in a gardener's cottage far from the palace.

From that day forward, peace reigned in that realm, and Gypsies were always made welcome there.

A donkey is a donkey, though laden with gold.

For nearly as long as there have been stories, there have been "Jack" stories. It is not surprising that Jack sometimes appears in Gypsy tales. Jack is usually portrayed as a resourceful young man, frequently living with his widowed mother, to whom he may be a help or a hindrance. In this Welsh story, Jack encounters a ghostly black dog, a staple in Welsh folklore. Other familiar motifs here are a contest between the hero and his adversary and the magic defeat of the dog.

The Black Dog

J ack and his mother lived in a cottage at the foot of a hill.

One night, as they sat at supper, they spied the new moon through a window. Being superstitious, Jack's mother said, "Jack, think now. We have seen the new moon through glass, so this month will be unlucky. We must be very careful."

Now, Jack was always careful. Many people in his neighborhood reported seeing ghosts of white ladies and mad monks, but he avoided such terrors by staying close to home.

The Black Dog

Jack was a great help to his mother. He gathered rushes to make rush candles and picked the wool which pastured sheep caught on hillside heather. In the autumn, he gathered hazelnuts and sold them. Each evening, he brought the cow to the cow-shed and penned up the ducks. But he was always careful to be home before dark.

One day, just a little before Christmas, Jack's mother said, "A cake would sit proud on our Christmas table."

Jack counted his savings and replied, "I'm off to the village to buy a mouth-watering Christmas cake full of sultanas and nuts!"

"This is not a lucky month," his mother reminded him.

But Jack was off to the village with money in his pocket and cake on his mind.

Jack had a warm welcome from the baker, for it was hard times. "We will all go hungry if it doesn't come better soon," the baker warned.

Jack wondered if he should keep his money in his pocket against starvation, but he had spoken for the cake and once he had spoken there was no going back.

Near the edge of the village, a few crafty boys offered pony rides cheap. Jack had his cake and a single coin left over and, though he was very keen on pony rides, he passed the boys by.

The wind was getting up and Jack felt chilly cold going over him. It was the season of short days and long nights, but Jack could have reached home before dark. Why he didn't was this: He came upon some Gypsy caravans and dallied to have his fortune told, spending his last coin. He learned only that the month would be unlucky for him.

When Jack started out again, a pale moon shone and the north wind rose. He clutched the Christmas cake and hurried along, happy he would soon be home.

But in the shadow of a ruined abbey, which lay beside the path Jack must tread, a huge black dog with eyes like fiery coals rose and stretched, then set out on the business of the night.

Back at Jack's cottage, his mother sat knitting stockings before the fireplace. Over the fire hung a pot of simmering rice and currants. From time to time, she glanced at the door, expecting to see her son bringing the Christmas cake.

Jack hurried along the path which wound up a gentle slope. When he reached the top, he would be able to look down upon his home.

When Jack passed the ruins of the old abbey, the great black dog trotted out behind him, the soft fall of its pawsteps muffled by the sound of Jack's boots on the stones.

As the boy neared the top of the slope, the dog drew abreast of him. Jack was startled, but when he saw his companion was only a black hound, he breathed a sigh of relief and patted the dog on the head.

Then Jack froze in terror, for his hand went through the dog's head as though through air. In that instant, he understood that it was no ordinary dog, but a ghost!

Jack's brain began to work. He set his legs in motion and ran as fast as he could.

The dark creature sprang forward with a roar and matched Jack step for step. As he ran, a rumbling growl sounded from his ghostly throat.

Jack threw a glance over his shoulder and caught sight of white teeth in a drawn-back mouth. Jack ran faster.

As the two reached the top of the hill, Jack saw his mother's cottage in the thin moonlight. Only a little farther, and he would be safe!

At this moment the terrible hound gathered himself to spring. He lunged at Jack and landed on top of the luckless boy. Jack nearly fainted from fright.

"Now I will devour you," the dog snarled.

Jack tried hard to think, but he had not been in a fix like this before. "Do your worst," he gasped, "but take this cake to my mother so she will have a happy Christmas."

The ghost-dog's heart was touched just a little. "How is your mother?" he asked the surprised boy.

"Keeping pretty well, some days better than others," Jack stammered.

The dog nodded sympathetically. "These are hard times," he said. "People are dying who have never died before."

For a minute or two, Jack thought that the dark hound would let him go. But things were not that simple.

"For the sake of your mother, I will not devour you right away," the dog considered. "Let us have a match of wrestling and if you win, which you cannot do, I will leave you alone."

They declared it a bargain.

Jack started the Christmas cake on it's own, down the hill to the cottage. It rolled on for a little, wobbled crazily, and fell over, sliding the rest of the way on the path.

Then the match began.

The dog caught Jack's arm in his massive jaws and forced him to the ground. Jack was so frightened that his strength was doubled and he tore free. But the huge dog took Jack's collar in his teeth and shook poor Jack like a ragbag.

It seemed to Jack that the battle went on for hours. The great dog was fierce and powerful, but Jack, driven by desperation, was able to hold him off. As the dog drew back on its haunches for a final spring, he uttered deep night-noises, sounding like thunder.

Jack shivered and retreated, trying frantically to reach safety. In a final burst of energy, the boy turned and raced to the foot of the hill. But the beast was after him in a flash, and flung himself on top of Jack. The two lay in a heap outside the cottage.

"This is no fair contest and I must get what help I can," Jack realized. He forced himself from under the huge paws of the dog and pounded on the cottage window. If his mother came with the broom, she could clout the dog on the head and drive him off, Jack thought. He well knew the strength of his mother when armed with her broom!

As she sat knitting, Jack's mother heard knocking at the window and looked up to see her son's face pressed against the glass.

"Why, it's Jack!" she cried. "He's having a bit of fun with me." She rose and gave the rice a stir, knowing her son would be hungry for his supper.

When he failed to make his mother see his desperate situation, Jack gave up all hope of being rescued.

"I'll give this beast one thing to remember me by," he resolved. He drew back and struck a mightly blow with all his strength on the dog's muzzle.

In that instant, the dog's enormous head flew from its body. With a roar, the head vanished. The headless body shuddered, stretched to its full length, and loped away up the hill, disappearing over the crest.

Jack located his cake, and went to greet his mother. He was worn out. His cake was broken, his coat in tatters, and his cap lost.

After that night, Jack stayed close to home. He milked the cow, fed the ducks, and warned everybody who crossed his path to keep a sharp lookout for a terrible ghost dog.

In this age of automobiles, the hills and valleys in those parts can be crossed safely at any hour. But some say, from time to time on a moonlight night, the terrible headless hound lies in wait for heedless travelers.

Never buy a handkerchief or choose a wife by candlelight.

The Devil makes frequent appearances in Gypsy tales.
In this one, he is outwitted by a clever old woman
who owns a coveted magic kettle. Self-filling cooking
pots are found in folktales of many lands, and the theft
of such magic objects usually results in considerable
trouble for the thief.

The Kettle Which Filled Itself

There was an old Gypsy woman named
Zara, who had a magic kettle. This was
in the rosy early morning of the world,
when enchantment was all around.

Zara left her life on the road and settled in a
little stone cottage at the edge of the sea. There she
dwelled with her kettle, which filled itself with thick, rich soup
whenever it was emptied.

One night, the Devil himself came over the sea in a small
boat, for he smelled the soup and a hungry eye can see a long
way.

"What are we going to eat this night?" the Devil asked, marching straight into Zara's cottage.

"I do not know what you are going to eat, but I am going to have fresh bread and soup," said Zara, cutting a thick slice from a newly-baked loaf.

Now the Devil was a bread-eater and a soup-lover. He watched each bite Zara took.

"Stop staring at me like a big-eyed rabbit!" Zara ordered. She shoved the Devil from the cottage, shut the door, and settled down to sleep.

After a little while, the Devil stole quietly back into the cottage and crept up to the kettle, which to his amazement, was once again full.

Zara sprang from her bed and snatched up a broom, driving the Devil back from the table.

"Run for your life, soup thief!" she shouted.

She chased the Devil around and around, finally driving him from the cottage and out into the night.

The Devil clambered up a tree, certain Zara could not follow him there. He perched among the branches.

But the Devil did not know all there was to know about Zara. He did not know that she was a witch, who could cause milk to sour, raise storms, and bring on several kinds of disasters.

"Now I will give you something to think about, soup thief!" she called up to the Devil.

Lightning flashed and thunder boomed. Rain beat down, drenching the Devil. Satisfied, Zara returned to the cottage, barred the door, and went to sleep.

"That is no ordinary old woman, and that is no ordinary kettle," the Devil snarled. "I will get that kettle, one way or another."

Next morning, when Zara went out to feed her ducks, the Devil was waiting anxiously for her.

"Don't hop around here like your shoes are full of snakes. Go about your business," Zara snapped.

The Devil craned his neck and stared through the open door. The kettle was on the table and it was full of steaming soup. "It will be a simple matter to coax that old woman away, then to snatch that kettle," thought the Devil.

He waited until Zara went back into the cottage. Then he opened the gate of the duck pen and chased the ducks out among the trees.

The Devil rapped smartly on the cottage door.

"Your ducks have broken free and all my efforts to capture them have failed," he announced. Then he waited for Zara to step out of the cottage.

Zara did not step out. Instead, she called, "Come ducks, come," and the ducks gathered together and hurried into the pen. The last one closed the gate behind him.

The Devil sat brooding over his situation. He was growing very hungry. He wanted that kettle and the soup that was in it.

Evening came. The Devil peered in the cottage window and saw Zara at her meal. Zara saw the Devil's nose pressed against the window and his silver saucer-eyes staring at her.

"If you will come outside, I will show you a hairy beast that is trampling your garden," the Devil called.

"I do not care about a hairy beast. Go away!" Zara shouted.

The Kettle Which Filled Itself

The Devil settled under a tree for the night and thought how he could frighten Zara into leaving her cottage. Then he changed his notion altogether and smiled slyly as he made a clever plan.

Next morning the Devil gathered a fistful of flowers and presented himself at Zara's door. "I fear you have misjudged me," he said, giving the flowers to Zara. "If you will walk with me, I can clear up this misunderstanding."

Zara was suspicious, but she was also curious, so she went with him. Their way wound among the greening trees, where birds trilled joyously.

"Sit here on this mossy stone and close your eyes, while I ask you a very important question," the Devil instructed.

Now Zara was certain she knew the question the Devil would ask. She closed her eyes and imagined the power she would have as Missus Devil.

Meanwhile, the Devil imagined the everlasting supply of delicious soup he would have as owner of the magic kettle.

Zara waited.

After a few minutes, she thought it would do no harm to peep, so she opened one eye a little. There was the Devil, creeping toward the cottage.

Zara rose with a whoop and sped after him.

The Devil heard her coming, flung open the cottage door and shot in, seizing the kettle.

Zara lunged at him and for a long minute the two struggled over the kettle, but Zara wrenched it away, spilling soup all over the Devil.

The kettle refilled itself at once. Then the Devil was more

determined than ever to possess it.

"You will never lure me from this cottage again, false friend!" Zara shrieked, finally pushing the Devil out the door.

That night there came to the Devil a notion so clever that he jumped up and down with delight.

"If I cannot take that old woman from her cottage, I will take the cottage from her!" he declared.

As Zara slept inside the cottage, the Devil set to work by the light of the moon. He removed stones from the cottage, one by one, beginning at the front door, working quickly and quietly.

After a little while, half the cottage was gone. Asleep, Zara felt the chilly night air and pulled the covers close around her.

At last the kettle stood revealed, shining in the moonlight. The Devil reached through the hole in the wall and seized the kettle. Then he ran as fast as he could through the trees to the shore, where his small boat was tied.

By the time the cold air awakened Zara and she realized what had happened, the Devil had put out to sea.

Zara ran to the shore and raised a fearsome storm. Wind sprang up and lightning knifed down the western sky. Thunder boomed. But the Devil sailed on, spooning soup into his hungry mouth.

Now, a kettle which fills itself is not to be trifled with and this kettle had a thought or two of its own. Old Zara stood on the shore and here was the kettle being carried out to sea, where it did not belong.

The kettle began to fill. It filled and it filled until it overflowed. The Devil spooned as fast as he could, but he was no match for the kettle.

The boat filled with soup and sank among the waves, but the kettle bobbed back to shore and Zara's waiting arms.

The Devil made his way to a distant land, where he continued his disagreeable career. But the memory of Zara's magic kettle never ceased troubling him.

Luck be on you.

From Wales comes another "Jack" story. Jack Apple, despair of the village but pride of his mother, encounters a ghostly hunt and a terrible green man. Such hunts, which were thought to fly through the air or course just above the ground, have been told of in Britain for centuries. They are variously believed to be fallen angels or mortals who have died.

The Green Man, celebrated in folklore of Britain, represents man's oneness with the earth. He is sometimes portrayed as jovial; sometimes menacing. Representations of him are found in stone on great cathedrals and in such familiar stories as "Jack and the Beanstalk."

Jack and the Green Man

Young Jack Apple lived with his widowed mother in a cozy cottage hard by a village cobbler shop.

Jack's mother kept a few chickens on a patch of poor land and brought in a living by selling eggs. Jack had no interest in work. Instead, he went on long rambling walks about the countryside to see what he could see.

The Fish Bride

Neighbors declared Jack an idler, but his mother always spoke up for him: "Jack will go far in this world, but he will always come again," she would say.

To make matters worse, Jack's friends worked hard and from their earnings bought fine presents for their mothers. There were shawls and brooches and copper pots.

"You have raised a worthless rolling stone and one fine day he will leave for good," the neighbors all said.

"Jack will always come again," his mother said firmly.

One day, wanting money for sweets, Jack took a job of work at a sheepwalk near the village. Things went his way for a while, but the day grew hot and he drank all the water from the flask at his belt.

The sheep climbed higher and Jack with them, until they reached the top of a high hill. While the sheep grazed, Jack stretched out on the ground and napped.

Jack awoke with a start to see that the sun had disappeared below the horizon. At that very moment, the ghostly hunt, a pack of horsemen in full cry, came thundering through the sky, mounted on pitch black horses and followed by huge black hounds. The hooves of the horses skimmed the high rocks and the dogs bayed.

Jack stared in amazement. All his life he had heard tales of ghostly huntsmen, but he doubted the truth of those stories. Now here was that company of spirits racing over his head, the riders hallooing.

Suddenly, without a thought of the consequences, Jack grasped the flying tail of the largest horse and hung on. Far below, the sheep stared up at him. The roofs of the village faded in the distance.

As unexpectedly as it had begun, the wild ride ended. Jack found himself standing alone in a strange place and he didn't like the look of things.

All around him, as far as he could see, stretched a garden. Trees with twisted trunks were dark as clouds overhead and great arched ferns cast green shadows. Winged insects darted over the grass. There were no paths through the hedges. Jack looked around at the strange garden in the fading twilight and shivered.

"I believe I have made a mistake," he thought.

Then night was on him.

Jack saw a light flickering in the distance. "There may be supper ahead," he thought hopefully, hastening toward the light.

An old woman answered Jack's rap at her cottage door.

"You look to be a proper young gentleman," she said. "What are you doing in this place?"

"This might surprise you one way or another, but I don't know where I am," Jack confessed. "But I do know I am hungry."

The old woman set Jack to work on bread and cheese.

"I would thank you for a drink of water, since my flask is empty," Jack said.

"There is only rainwater for my drink and it has not rained in days," the old woman told him.

"How is the garden watered when there is no rain?" Jack asked.

The old woman motioned for Jack to be still.

"The terrible Green Man, who is squire here, drinks and waters the garden from a magic spring which rises beneath an oak tree. You must not let him find you here, for he eats strangers who pass this way."

Jack was frightened, but curious.

"I will drink from that magic spring before I leave this place tomorrow," he declared.

"Tomorrow is not tomorrow," the old woman said. "This garden is outside time and a day here is a year elsewhere. I strayed here and have come to like it, but I advise you to leave if you can."

The old woman feared the Green Man would find Jack at her cottage and punish them both.

"I wish you luck, now go away," she told Jack.

Jack crept through the garden, listening for the terrible Green Man. As he clambered over a hedge, he pricked his finger. A single drop of blood fell on the petal of a white rose.

Jack slept that night in a bed of willow shoots. "Tomorrow," he thought, "I will find a way to return home."

Next morning, as Jack slept, the Green Man walked in the garden and spied the blood on the rose. Then he found Jack.

Jack awoke in terror to find himself in the huge hands of the Green Man. He was hoisted by the collar of his coat and his legs swung helplessly in the air.

The Green Man was covered from head to feet with foliage, so he resembled a tower of leaves. His eyes were fiery coals and his mouth was a cavern, large enough to swallow Jack. The Green Man lowered Jack slowly to his open mouth.

"Wait, you cannot eat me!" Jack cried.

"Why not?" the Green Man roared.

Jack tried frantically to think.

"It would not be sporting. You must give me a fair chance to save my life!"

The Green Man snarled angrily, but declared it a bargain. "If you pick all the beans in the garden by sundown, I will spare your life," he said. "If you fail, you will become my supper."

Now Jack was not a worker, but he was determined to pick all the beans and save his skin. There were three long rows of beans and three baskets. Jack set to work with a will, filling the first basket.

The Green Man rested beneath an oak tree, and beyond him was the spring the old woman had told Jack about.

Jack worked rapidly, filling the first basket, then he started on the second row.

The Green Man watched Jack, chuckling.

When the second basket was filled, Jack went on to the final row. The sun was directly overhead and he was very hungry.

All around were luscious fruits: figs and pomegranates and dusky grapes. The Green Man ate a pomegranate and drank from the spring, but Jack dared not stop picking beans.

When he finished the third row, Jack stood up to look at the three full baskets. Then he saw that the rows were once again heavy with beans and the baskets were empty.

"The beans have come again!" Jack cried.

The Green Man roared with laughter. He lay back on the grass, his head pillowed on a mossy rock.

Jack began again. He worked feverishly, but the faster he picked, the faster the bean rows filled again.

"I have always believed no good comes from working," Jack thought sourly. He stole a glance at the Green Man, who had been silent for some time. The Green Man's eyes were closed.

"Could he be asleep?" Jack wondered.

Jack decided to take a chance. He summoned all his nerve and stole silently past the Green Man, who did not open his eyes or move.

Jack sped lightly across the grass and filled his flask at the spring. Then he set off quickly to the cottage of the old woman.

"So you have come again," the old woman said.

"It seems so," Jack replied. "I have outwitted the Green Man and taken water from the magic spring. Now I will go home."

"How will you do that?" the old woman asked.

At that very instant, Jack heard the thundering hooves of the ghostly hunt.

"I'll go as I came!" he cried. He caught the flying tail of the last horse, and was gone.

Back in the village, a year had passed. Jack's mother stood at the gate of her cottage. She saw Jack walking down the high hill of the sheepwalk, where he had left the ghostly hunt.

"Jack has come again!" she cried happily.

All the neighbors who had declared Jack an idiot came out to meet him.

"I have brought you a present," Jack told his mother. And

he took the top from his flask and sprinkled water from the magic spring on the poor plot of land before the cottage.

In an instant, the patch of soil bloomed, becoming a magnificent garden. Tall trees sprang from lush grass and hedges ringed the cottage. Fragrance of fruit and flowers filled the air. Wind played leafy boughs like a harp. Unlike the garden out of time, where the Green Man ruled, this garden was good.

Jack and his mother lived happily in the midst of the garden, and all the neighbors pronounced Jack a fine fellow.

The forest is safer than the marketplace.

In this tale, a foolish girl upsets her friends by "crying wolf" too many times. Set in Wales, it contains traditional elements of Celtic folklore. A spinning fairy offers the girl three opportunities to make a fortune, but the girl fails to recognize the magic all about her.

Biddy Oak

A foolish dairymaid called Biddy Oak thought she would have a bit of sport with her friends by pretending to see a strange sight in the sky.

"Look there!" she cried. "See the coaches lined up like a train, moving through the clouds!"

The others saw nothing, but believed Biddy must have the gift of seeing into another world.

This made Biddy feel very important, so she pretended to see more things.

"Look there!" she would shout. "A creature is peeping from beneath the chair!"

Of course no one saw anything.

Biddy Oak

Days passed and Biddy's stories grew more frightening.

"When I was bringing in the cows, I heard something coming after me—clank, clank, clank—rattling its chains," she reported.

Soon all of Biddy's friends were afraid to go about their work, but huddled in chimney corners, trembling.

One night, Biddy leapt from her bed crying, "Hark! A terrible one-eyed monster with a long forked tongue is coming to eat us up!"

This was too much for Biddy's friends. The story was so ridiculous that they saw at once they had been fools to believe anything Biddy said. Since Biddy had made them feel foolish, she must go. In the middle of the night, by the light of the moon, they turned her out.

Now Biddy was out of a situation. She set off down the road, taking with her an extra petticoat, three oatcakes, and a pot of honey, which was all she owned in the world. As the next night fell, she came to a greenwood and there saw a lady clad in green, spinning flax in the moonshine.

"I saw you coming a long way off, Biddy Oak," the lady said.

"Then you must know my sad story, how my friends have turned me out for naught," Biddy replied.

Biddy thought herself clever, but the lady was not deceived. "You tricked your friends, but my heart is moved by foolish girls, so I will help you," the lady said.

Biddy did not like to be reminded of her faults.

"Before the next new moon, I will give you three chances

to make your fortune, Biddy Oak. If you do, you can return to your friends and share your good luck with them and they will forgive you."

Biddy did not doubt the words of the lady, for such occurrences were usual at that time.

"Be off with you and keep a sharp eye out, for you will have only three chances," the lady warned.

Biddy slept that night in a sweetgrass meadow, then set out to find her fortune. Before long, she met a tinker pulling an empty cart. By smooth words and an oatcake, Biddy persuaded the tinker to give her the cart.

"This may be the beginning of my fortune," she thought.

But the cart seemed to be only the kind of cart that can be seen any day. It was heavy to pull and one of its wheels wobbled. Biddy soon became convinced she had made a mistake.

Then it happened that Biddy saw a fair ahead, where people were buying and selling. "Here's a chance to sell this worthless cart and gain something of value," she thought.

Biddy looked at the flocks of sheep and geese and fine ponies stamping on the turf. But those were beyond her means, so she traded her cart to a goatboy for one of his goats.

The goatboy gave the wobbling cartwheel a great *thwack!* with a mallet to mend it, and to Biddy's amazement, the cart immediately filled to overflowing with gold coins.

Then Biddy knew the tinker and the cart had been the work of the spinning lady and that she had lost the first of her three chances at fortune.

"Two chances are left to me, and you may be one of them," Biddy told the goat.

But the goat seemed to be only the kind of goat that can be seen any day.

Up and down the countryside they went, Biddy and the goat. They ate from orchards and slept under the stars. Thistles caught on Biddy's skirts and brambles tangled her hair, as she watched for a sign of fortune.

It happened one day that Biddy came to a treacherous bog. Rain was falling. The goat planted his feet on the edge of the bog and would not be moved. He rolled over with his feet in the air.

Biddy pinched and pulled the goat, then gave him a mighty shove into the bog. In an instant, the goat vanished and in his place a gleaming white pony with a silver bridle-rein rose from the bog. It ran like the wind and in a moment was out of sight.

"Goat, you deceived me!" Biddy shouted, seeing her second chance at fortune disappear over the hills.

Now it happened there lived at that time, under a hill near the bog, an old woman skilled in magic. She did not like foolish girls.

Biddy tapped on the old woman's door, seeking shelter from the rain. When she related the story of the spinning lady and the three chances for fortune, the old woman saw an opportunity to trick Biddy.

"I will give you a fortune you need not search for, since you are a fine girl," she promised falsely. "Believe me and trust no other."

The old woman's smooth words pleased Biddy.

"Take this pallet with you and cushion your head upon it tonight. When you awake, you will have a surprise."

At the door of the old woman's home there was a smooth white stone. As she passed, Biddy kicked it from her path and it became a beautiful bird with a jeweled tail. It rose into the air and hovered long enough for Biddy to catch it, but she did not. She kept tight hold on the pallet the old woman had given her.

"That must have been the last of the three chances, but I do not care," Biddy thought. "The spinning lady obliged me to work for a fortune. The old woman is my true friend and appreciates me."

Biddy slept that night with the pallet under her head, but when she awoke, she found the pallet gone and a toadstool in its place.

Biddy turned matters over and over in her mind, realizing the wily old woman had tricked her. Then she remembered how she had tricked her friends, frightening them and making them feel foolish. She determined to return to her friends and explain to them that she had learned a thing or two.

She started for home, going down and down twisting lanes and by a long uphill way so she would not meet the spinning lady, who would be sure to call her a fool. She had plenty of time to repent her dishonest ways as she went. When at last she arrived home, her friends welcomed her, letting old quarrels go, as friends do. But Biddy never told the story of all that had befallen her, for she was certain they would not believe her.

Acorns were good until bread was found.

This tale from Wales was no doubt intended to warn against cheating or scorning a Gypsy. In the story, a rich man, believing a Gypsy means to cheat him, cheats her, then comes to grief.

The Haunted Inn

One day, a rich man of business named Spratt met a fortuneteller in the street.

"Your fortune for a silver coin," the fortuneteller offered.

"It is a bargain!" Spratt declared.

The fortuneteller spun out Spratt's future, then stretched out her palm for payment.

Spratt only laughed and passed on.

The fortuneteller called after him: "Here is a riddle for you. How soon will a man who cheats the fortuneteller be struck down?"

In only minutes, Spratt found himself enveloped by a dense fog. Although he knew the street well, he became confused.

He fancied he heard voices all about him, whispering his name. He pushed on in earnest, but he was uneasy.

Now, as it happened, the fog cleared for an instant and Spratt saw the door of an inn where he was sure no inn had stood before.

He made up his mind to rest there a bit until the fog cleared, so he pulled the bell rope. An old man opened the inn door.

"Welcome to you Squire Spratt," he said. "Aren't you lucky to find a nice warm place on this foggy afternoon?"

Now, what puzzled Spratt was this: How did the old man know his name?

"You will be wanting to rest and then have dinner," the old man continued.

"Lead on!" Spratt commanded.

So it was that Spratt found himself in a small candlelit room up the stairs at the end of a dark, narrow passage.

In the room were a bed, a well-appointed writing desk, a candlestand, and one small window. Spratt placed his hat and coat upon a peg, blew out the candle, and prepared to rest.

No sooner had he done this than an inkstand from the writing desk whizzed past his ear.

Spratt sprang up, alarmed. But, believing it to be a freak occurrence, he resumed his rest.

In an instant, he was tumbled from the bed and turned head over heel. He landed *bump!* on the floor.

Spratt looked around to see who had set upon him, but there was nobody.

Suddenly he found himself in the air again and it was all he could do to stay right side up. An unseen hand snatched Spratt's money purse from his waistcoat pocket and scattered coins about the floor. Spratt scrambled after them.

He crouched beneath the writing desk, clutching his money, but the desk moved and so did the bed. They whirled around and around.

Then the voices began. They were shrill and it seemed to Spratt they were coming from inside the walls. The whole room was full up with mischief, and there he was, an important, respectable man, plagued by dark, unseen forces.

Spratt made his way past the whirling bed to the window, looking for a way to escape. The writing desk blocked his passage to the door. As he raised the window, he felt the force of hands pushing him out. Spratt clung to the sash, managing to save himself.

A path was now clear to the door. Spratt raced to it, but the door was locked. He began to shout for help.

After some time, the door opened.

"I heard a cry of distress," the old man said. "What is the matter?"

"You must save my life," Spratt cried, clinging to him. "This room is haunted!"

Then Spratt looked behind him: All in the room was in its proper place. He was hard put to understand what had happened.

"Let us proceed to your meal," the old man suggested, ushering the bewildered Spratt out the door.

The Fish Bride

The dining chamber was dimly lit. In the center of the room was a table set for five. Four diners sat at the table.

Spratt squinted to see who his dinner companions were. They rose to greet him and he saw, to his horror, that they were his own dear aunties, who were forty years dead!

Off and away went Spratt, leaving the terrible inn behind as fast as he could. But in aftertimes, Spratt was fair in his dealings, especially with fortunetellers he chanced to meet in the street!

Plenty of luck to sell, but none to keep.

Here is the widow Sophie's son, Marco, who is
determined to find fame and fortune, in the tradition
of daring young men celebrated in various cultures.
Marco takes on a challenging task and uses the
Gypsy's love of the open road to triumph.

King of
the Moon

The widow Sophie's son, Marco, who
will never be forgotten, awoke one
morning to find that winter had come
during the night. All the countryside
was frosted like a bridal cake. This was at a time
when the caravan was in Russia, near the city of
Minsk.

Viktor Petrovich, Marco's new friend from the town,
looked in at the doorway.

"I have borrowed a sleigh from my uncle," Viktor announced. "Let us set out on an adventure."

"Wolves will eat you up on your way," Sophie warned. "Only fools would travel on such a day."

Marco pulled on his coat. "I am certain I am destined to become rich and famous and this may be the day fortune finds me!" he crowed.

Marco seated himself in the sleigh and Viktor took up the reins.

"I know what I am doing," Marco called back to his mother.

"Humph!" replied Sophie.

Marco hunched beneath the sheepskin robe. Viktor clutched the reins with frozen fingers. They stamped their toes to keep them warm.

The sleigh ran smoothly over snowy hills and past small villages. Marco and Viktor waved gaily at villagers and talked excitedly of adventures they might have.

The day wore on. The wind rose and the temperature fell. Marco and Viktor shivered and their breath came in clouds.

"This was *your* big idea!" Marco accused Viktor.

"*You* did not object," Viktor pointed out.

Soon they came to an inn at the side of the road. Viktor pulled the sleigh over, sighing, "The storm is growing worse and night will soon fall. We had better stay here until morning."

When they had made provisions for their horse and sleigh and settled themselves before a fire in the inn, Marco and Viktor faced a dilemma.

"How will we pay for our lodging?" Marco whispered.

"We will think about that when we have thawed our fingers and toes," Viktor hissed.

A dark-cloaked man hovered nearby. He approached Marco and Viktor and spoke softly. "If you lack funds, perhaps I can assist you," he said.

"Why would you do that?" Marco asked suspiciously.

The stranger pulled up a chair close to the fire and settled himself in it.

"I am a minister of the czar," he confided.

Marco laughed rudely.

"I, myself, am the Emperor of China," he said. "My companion is the Sultan of Turkey."

Marco and Viktor laughed.

The stranger waited until they paused for breath, then said solemnly, "I am telling you the truth. I am searching for a clever, courageous young man who will perform a service for the czar. The reward for success will be a royal title. Perhaps one of you will undertake the task?"

Marco leapt up, his eyes wide.

"If what you say is true, your search is over," he declared. "I am that clever, courageous young man you have been looking for."

Viktor tugged at Marco's sleeve.

"Are you mad?" he demanded. "You have not even heard what task you must perform."

"I have already told you that my destiny is to become rich and famous," Marco assured him. He turned to the stranger. "Lead on!" he commanded.

Marco and Viktor traveled with the minister of the czar for several days, enjoying the finest accommodations. At length, they arrived at the magnificent court of the czar and stood before the czar himself. Viktor trembled from head to toe, but Marco stood proudly.

When the czar heard the minister's story, he addressed Marco.

"My minister will explain the task you are to perform, and if you succeed, a royal title will be your reward," he declared.

The czar's minister hurried the young men away, and then explained to Marco the problem which needed to be solved.

"Just across the river stands a beautiful palace which once belonged to Tasha the Terrible, cousin of the czar. Unfortunately, it was won from Countess Tasha in a game of chance by a huge fierce fellow who refuses to give it back. The law is on his side. The countess plagues the czar day and night, demanding that he return the palace to her. It will be your task to remove this fellow in order that the Countess Tasha may live there again."

"I can do that!" Marco boasted. "My good friend Viktor Petrovich will accompany me."

"Me?" Viktor shrieked. "Why should I do such a foolish thing?"

But Marco persuaded his friend that all would be well. That night, as they lay awake in the czar's palace awaiting morning and their adventure, he spoke confidently.

"That royal title is as good as mine," he boasted.

Next day, Marco and Viktor, bundled to their chins, crossed the frozen river and climbed a hill to the grand palace of the countess. They placed their weight against the iron gates and swung them wide.

Before Marco could lift the massive knocker, the door creaked open and a huge man loomed over them.

"What do you want here?" the man boomed.

"We are poor travelers who have lost our way and need shelter from the cold," Marco whined, making a pitiful face.

The huge fellow scowled, but stepped aside and motioned for them to enter.

"Perhaps you will offer us a hot drink?" Marco suggested boldly.

Viktor rolled his eyes in despair. "What will you dare next?" he whispered.

Soon, the three sat before a fire, sipping hot drinks. Marco studied the man's face, looking for something familiar there.

"You aren't really such a terrible fellow," Viktor blurted out.

"What do you mean by that?" the man demanded.

"My friend only meant that owners of such grand palaces are often haughty and greedy," Marco hurriedly explained.

The man laughed good-naturedly.

"I have not always lived in this manner. I won this palace in a game of chance. Let me show it to you."

As their host led them through long corridors and spacious rooms, Marco whispered to Viktor. "There is something familiar about this fellow and I must learn if my guess is correct."

Marco addressed the man. "I wonder sir, if you would tell us your name?"

"Certainly," their host replied. "I am Yanko, and have been so all my life."

Marco smiled slyly, a plan forming in his brain.

"It happens the Countess Tasha wants me to return this palace to her, and I will not give it up," Yanko continued.

"Never?" Marco asked innocently.

"Not ever!" Yanko roared.

Marco and Viktor spent the night in a luxurious bedchamber, as guests of Yanko.

"This should prove to you that I am destined for fame and fortune," Marco told Viktor. "We have traveled in comfort with the czar's minister, been guests of the czar himself, and now rest in this palatial estate. All this has happened to you because you are my friend."

"The adventure is not over," Viktor pointed out. "Who knows what disaster may yet befall us?"

Next morning, Marco sought out Yanko and prepared to put his plan into operation. He greeted his host warmly.

"I have only now realized that I know you," said Marco. "I saw you once at a fair and heard you play your fiddle. Your music was magnificent. How tragic it is that you are now the victim of treachery."

"Treachery? What treachery?" Yanko roared.

Marco paced the room, his voice mournful.

"It is so clear to me that the game of chance you won was the result of a clever plan. The plotters ensured that you would be caged here, unable to pose a threat to their power. This grand house is no more than a prison and you are a prisoner. Oh, it is all so tragic."

"Why would anyone do such a thing?" Yanko demanded.

"You are known far and wide as a leader of Gypsies. You are a chief; a KING! You were once powerful, but now you are here, a pitiful figure. It is more than I can bear." Marco pretended to brush a tear from his eye.

Yanko sat brooding.

"I was once important," he conceded.

"Of course you were," Marco said heartily. "When I think of the long road, the wide sky, and the freedom of the caravan compared to this pile of stone, I could weep for you."

Viktor sniffed.

"Why, I'll wager your fiddle is not far from where we stand," Marco cried. He scurried about the room, pulling out drawers and opening cupboards. At last, he discovered a violin and held it aloft, victoriously.

"Play for us," he urged, offering the instrument to Yanko.

Yanko raised the violin and drew the bow across it. Music filled the room and Marco smiled at Viktor.

"Am I not a genius?" he whispered.

At last the music ended and Marco pretended to despair.

"What a cruel plot has imprisoned you here, away from the wind and the rain; away from those friends who loved your music!"

"Who is responsible for this terrible deed?" Yanko demanded.

"Why, it must have been the czar."

"I see it all!" Yanko roared, rushing about, gathering a warm coat and provisions. "I will return to the road, the only true life!"

Marco and Viktor watched Yanko dance down the road, then put on their coats and started across the frozen river. As they walked, they speculated about the royal title Marco would receive.

"I will probably be made a count and receive gold and jewels." Marco guessed.

"Gold and jewels?" Viktor asked in surprise. "I did not know there would be gold and jewels. Do not forget that I was at your side throughout the ordeal."

Braving freezing winds and blowing snow, Marco and Viktor arrived at last at the court and stood once more before the czar. A crowd had gathered to see the young man who had freed the palace. The people craned their necks to get a glimpse of Marco, smirking at his ragged coat and broken hat.

"Ask about the gold and jewels," Viktor prompted.

The czar spoke.

"You were promised a royal title and it shall be yours," he said.

The crowd hushed, awaiting the announcement.

Marco held his breath.

"Henceforth, you will be known as King of the Moon!" the czar proclaimed.

The crowd roared with laughter.

"He has tricked you! He has made a fool of you!" Viktor whispered.

"Each night, when the moon appears in the sky, all men will behold your realm. Have you nothing to say?" the czar asked, beaming at Marco.

Marco sighed and looked about the crowd. Then he addressed the czar.

"I do have something to say. Perhaps it has come to your attention that I am a Gypsy."

"Of course I know that. Do you think me a fool?" the czar snapped.

"Then you will also realize I must preserve the honor of my people by repaying your insult. I am forced to place upon you, and all the members of your court, a particularly unpleasant Gypsy curse."

The crowd drew back in horror.

The czar started to rise, then sank down in his seat, his eyes wide.

Marco smiled sweetly.

"I am afraid you can do nothing to prevent this. You brought it on yourself."

"Do something!" the czar ordered his minister.

Marco whispered to Viktor. "Suggest a reward."

"Per-perhaps a reward?" Viktor croaked.

"What's that you say?" the czar demanded.

"A reward," Viktor repeated, his voice shaking.

Marco pretended to consider. "If you insisted, I might be persuaded to accept a bag of gold coins for my service," he offered.

"There would be no curse?" the czar asked anxiously.

"There will be no curse," Marco agreed.

So it was that Marco and Viktor Petrovich traveled in style, staying at the finest inns and dining on delicacies, on their way home.

"Perhaps you should have placed a Gypsy curse on the czar to teach him a lesson," Viktor said.

"Do you know any Gypsy curses?" Marco asked.

"Of course not, but you do," Viktor replied.

Marco shook his head.

"None," he said. "It is not a curse, but the fear of curses which causes people to tremble. Remember always, it takes a trickster to outwit a trickster."

When Marco arrived home, no coins were left in his bag. His mother met him in the doorway.

"Sit down and I will tell you the wonderful story of how I outwitted the czar, spent a bagful of gold, and became King of the Moon," he said to her.

"Humph!" the widow Sophie replied.

The darkness of the forest is the light of the Gypsies.

Tales of captivity date from ancient times, one of the earliest being the Greek myth of Persephone. Celtic folklore, with its roots in Celtic mythology, magic, and enchantment, frequently tells of mortals being taken captive by fairies. These mortals were required to serve as bond-slaves or to impart musical knowledge. This tale, which originated in Wales and reflects the Gypsies' dread of captivity, draws upon Celtic lore. The harp was present in many ancient societies, but has become an important symbol in Celtic countries. Gypsies frequently adopted the musical instruments of the lands in which they lived.

The Gypsy Harper

In the long ago, there was a Gypsy harper whose father was the wind and whose mother was the sea. He was the keeper of the Gypsies' souls. His songs explained how all things had begun.

The harpist's harp had been born in a flash of lightning. It echoed the heartbeat of the earth and its powers were threefold.

The Gypsy Harper

Music from the harp could heal, cause mystic sleep, and summon rain.

Neither the harp nor the harper had magical skill when apart from each other.

The harper and the Gypsies journeyed from place to place, and then came one day to a land where a cruel king reigned. The king saw the Gypsies and determined to put them to work in his fields. But he knew he must separate the harper from the other Gypsies, for he saw that the harper was the leader. So he invited the harper to the palace to play for him.

Now the harper possessed magic, but that could be conquered by cunning. He went with his harp up to the palace, where they played such sweet airs that the king grew wild with envy. He gave the harper a poison draught which brought deep sleep but did not kill.

The harper fell to the floor in a swoon and was born away to a dungeon. The king carried the harp to his own chamber, where he attempted to play as sweetly as the harper.

The Gypsies watched for the harper's return, but the palace was silent, swallowed by the night. Around the palace a ring of fire sprang up, which the king had lighted each night to protect his court from enemies.

Next day, the Gypsies were forced from their caravans and put to work in the king's fields. Sentries were posted to prevent their escape.

The harper revived and was set to work in the scullery, but no matter how he toiled, all trace of his labor disappeared at once. Next day and the day after, it was the same. Each night, he sank deep into sleep.

The Fish Bride

In the king's hands, the harp played only dreary, doleful music.

Each day and night, the king kept the harp at his side, determined to coax beautiful melodies from it. But the harp withheld that beauty. At last, convinced that the harp was of no use, the king flung it to the floor one night and there it lay, forgotten.

That was the chance for which the harp had waited. When night fell and the palace was silent, the harp began to call to the harper. It murmured as softly as the faintest breeze in a tone only the harper could hear.

The harper heard its call. He crept from the dungeon and slipped up the winding stair. Here and there candles flickered, throwing grotesque shadows on the walls. Once he heard the pattering of footsteps behind him, but it died away.

The harper was led on by the call of the harp and he found it at last. It nestled like a bird in his arms and the two were united in power. The harp sang a song of the open road, of wind and leaf, strong and clear.

All in the palace were roused. The king led a search, but no trace could be found, for the harper had fled to the courtyard.

There, the ring of fire sprang high before him, as the searchers pressed close behind. Then the harp worked a magic. The king and searchers sank down in mystic sleep and lay like broken dolls. A soft rain fell, quenching the flames which barred the path to freedom.

The Gypsies had despaired, but they danced with joy when the harper appeared in their midst. As he sang of yesterdays and

tomorrows, the Gypsies passed the king's sentries, silent in mystic sleep. They were free once again.

*Eat while you can. Tomorrow you may
be on the run.*

Lallah, the littlest daughter and least likely heroine, sets out on a quest. In offering herself for the task, she becomes the connection between old and new times, and finds her true calling, which reflects the Gypsy love of story. Contained here are the elements of myth: an earthly paradise spoiled by evil; a Sower; a magician's spell; and a land where the elements dwell.

Lallah Pombo

I n the first days following the long darkness, the Sower laid a handful of rice on the wind. Then he dispatched the wind messengers to spread the news of the sowing and bid all who heard to come and tend the rice. This happened on a great plain, near a jungle.

A king went forth to establish order in the Riceland.

For a time, a powerful magician was employed at the king's court, but the day came when that magician was discharged for working dark magic. The magician was so angry that he went to a high hill overlooking the palace and loosed a bagful of curses on the wind. Then he flew to the moon on the wing of a bird.

The Fish Bride

The people of the Riceland scurried about, gathering the curses. But they were unable to capture one of those curses and it was the worst one of all. Because of it, no rain fell in the Riceland and all growing things withered.

It happened that three Gypsy families had come to live in the Riceland. They were musicians, dancers, and singers whose fame spread far and wide. But Lallah, the littlest daughter, did not sing, could not dance, and played no music of any kind.

"I am probably of no use at all," she said, and so it seemed.

The king called a great council in order to find a way of overcoming the magician's curse. Scholars consulted ancient scrolls, recalled history, and discussed mystical incantations that had once defeated curses. Young poets who had played glad songs in former times, languished in the galleries, their harps silent. But the Riceland had been brought down, and all the efforts of the sages and scholars to restore it were fruitless.

One who was not present at the council was Lallah, the littlest Gypsy daughter. She sat at a southern window, gazing out at the Riceland. The lamp had nearly spent its light and shadows filled the room.

"The land is dust and there is not a grain of rice in the bin. If only I could do something to help," Lallah said to her mother.

"There is nothing you can do, unless you can bring rain," her mother replied.

"Where does rain live?" Lallah asked.

"How could I know that?" her mother replied.

Lallah slept little that night, and in the morning, she declared she would go in search of rain in order to save the Riceland.

Lallah Pombo

At dawn, Lallah passed through the moon gate into a land without borders. Without direction, she trusted and walked on.

After many days, Lallah reached a city. There she explained her journey and was advised to sit near a group of students who received instruction from a master. This she did, but she did not hear where rain lived, so she moved on.

The countryside around the city was barren and the way across the parched ground difficult. Lallah struggled forward and at length reached a small village.

Explaining her journey once again, she was advised by villagers to sit in the marketplace, listening to stories told by merchants who traveled the world. This she did, and indeed, the merchants' tales were wondrous, but Lallah did not hear where rain lived, so she moved on.

Farther and farther Lallah ventured, thinking all the while of the Riceland and its people.

One morning, before the sun had risen, Lallah came upon a group of travelers who explained they were going out to seek the meaning of life. Lallah thought perhaps these travelers would know where rain lived, but when she listened to their stories, she heard only about laws and rules. She did not hear where rain lived, so she passed on.

Lallah had nearly given up hope of finding rain, when she emerged from a dense forest and stepped onto the shore of a great sea. The moon rose, sending a shining path over the water.

"I can go no farther," Lallah said, sinking down on the shore. She listened as the sea and the sky and the wind spoke stories to her, and she understood she had come to the home of the rain.

So it was that the Sower stood before her and listened as she told him of the Riceland's fall.

"Please sow rice again, then send rain to make it grow," Lallah urged.

"I sowed rice following the long darkness," the Sower said. "Those were old times, when magic sprang up every high-road. But these are new times. You are the link between the old and the new, because you have offered yourself to save the Riceland."

"I am no one," Lallah objected.

Then Lallah stretched forth her hand and received rice from the Sower.

"Sow this rice and rain will follow," the Sower said. "Then set out into the world, telling all of the wondrous tales you have heard, in the city, in villages, from travelers, and most of all here, where secrets of the world are whispered. You are not 'no one,' but a storyteller, and storytellers are true nobility."

The Riceland flourished once more, and Lallah, the littlest Gypsy daughter, followed a storyteller's road all the many years of her life.

The true way to be wise is to hear,
see, and bear in mind.

When you cut a Gypsy in ten pieces, you have not killed him, you have only made ten more Gypsies.

Further Resources

Books

Ficowski, Jerzy. *Sister of the Birds, and Other Gypsy Tales.* Illustrated by Charles Mikolaycak. Translated by Lucia M. Borski. Nashville: Abringdon, 1976. Folktales collected from Gypsies of Poland. Six fine tales by an eminent authority on Gypsy lore.

Fonseca, Isabel. *Bury Me Standing: The Gypsies and Their Journey.* New York: Vintage Books/A division of Random House, Inc., 1996. Scholarly account of Gypsy culture, engagingly presented. Firmly rooted in contemporary Europe.

Groome, Francis Hindes. *Gypsy Folk-Tales.* London: Hurst and Blackett, 1899. Reprint edition: Arno Press, 1977. Authoritative, but difficult to locate. Introduction includes material about Gypsy history and population distribution.

Hampton, John. *The Gypsy Fiddle and Other Tales Told by the Gypsies.* New York: Interlink Books, 1992. The brief introduction contains information about Gypies in Russia and a glossary furnishes some Gypsy terms.

Hunt, Bernice Kohn. *The Gypsies.* Indianapolis: Bobbs-Merrill, 1972. History, life, and customs of the Gypsies.

McDowell, Bart. *Gypsies, Wanderers of the World.* Illustrated by Bruce Dale. Washington, D.C.: National Geographic Society, 1970. National Geographic Special Publications. Includes colored maps and illustrations.

Strom, Yale. *Uncertain Roads: Searching for the Gypsies.* New York: Four Winds Press, 1993. Account of Rom in Europe today by an author who spent time with them.

Tong, Diane. *Gypsy Folk-Tales*. New York: Harcourt, Brace & Company, 1989. Introduction for adult readers, but many tales suitable for young readers. The stories are preceded by notes about their origin. Immaculate scholarship and sprightly tales by a foremost authority.

Wedeck, H.E. and Baskin, Wade. *Dictionary of Gypsy Life and Lore.* New York: Philosophical Library, Inc., 1973. Comprehensive reference. Includes expressions and proverbs.

Yates, Dora E. *A Book of Gypsy Folk-tales.* London: Phoenix House, 1948. Gypsy tales stylishly retold. Introduction contains information about Gypsy storytelling and storytellers.

Periodical

Journal of the Gypsy Lore Society
5607 Greenleaf Road
Cherverly, MD 20785

Website

The Patrin
patrin@geocities.com